Hurray for Barbara Park and the Junie B. Jones® books!

"Park, one of the funniest writers around . . . brings her refreshing humor to the beginning chapter-book set." —*Booklist*

"Park is simply hilarious."
—America Online's *The Book Report*

"Park has a wonderful ear for the dialogue of five-year-olds and an even better grasp of how their minds operate." —*Booklist*

"Park is truly a funny writer. Although Junie B. is a kindergartner, she's sure to make middle graders laugh out loud." —*School Library Journal*

"Junie's swarms of young fans will continue to delight in her unique take on the world. . . . A hilarious, first-rate read-aloud." —*Kirkus Reviews*

"Junie B. is a darling of the young-reader set."
—*USA Today*

"The honesty and inventiveness of this savvy kindergartner make the Junie B. books accessible and completely enjoyable." —*School Library Journal*

2

Laugh out loud with Junie B. Jones!

Check out Barbara Park's other great books, listed at the end of this book!

Junie B. Jones
and a
Little Monkey Business

BY BARBARA PARK

illustrated by
Denise Brunkus

A STEPPING STONE BOOK™

Random House New York

To Cal and Nate,
the cutest little monkeys
their grammy ever saw!

Copyright © 1993 by Barbara Park
Illustrations copyright © 1993 by Denise Brunkus

All rights reserved. Published in the United States by Random House Children's Books, a division of Random House, Inc., New York.

RANDOM HOUSE and colophon are registered trademarks and A STEPPING STONE BOOK and colophon are trademarks of Random House, Inc.
JUNIE B. JONES is a registered trademark of Barbara Park, used under license.

www.randomhouse.com/kids/junieb

Educators and librarians, for a variety of teaching tools, visit us at
www.randomhouse.com/teachers

Library of Congress Cataloging-in-Publication Data
Park, Barbara.
Junie B. Jones and a little monkey business / Barbara Park ;
illustrated by Denise Brunkus.
   p. cm. "A stepping stone book."
SUMMARY: Through a misunderstanding, Junie B. thinks that her new baby brother is really a baby monkey, and her report of this news creates excitement and trouble in her kindergarten class.
ISBN 978-0-679-83886-9 (pbk.) — ISBN 978-0-679-93886-6 (lib. bdg.)
[1. Babies—Fiction. 2. Brothers and sisters—Fiction. 3. Kindergarten—Fiction.
4. Schools—Fiction.] I. Brunkus, Denise, ill. II. Title.
PZ7.P2197Jt 1993 [Fic]—dc20 92-56706

Printed in the United States of America 52 51 50 49 48 47 46 45 44 43

Contents

1 / Surprise

My name is Junie B. Jones. The B stands for Beatrice. Except I don't like Beatrice. I just like B and that's all. B stands for something else, too.

B stands for B-A-B-Y.

I'm only in kindergarten. But I already know how to spell B-A-B-Y. That's because my mother told me that she is going to have one of those things.

She and Daddy told me about it at dinner one night. It was the night we had stewed tomatoes—which I hate very much.

"Daddy and I have a surprise for you, Junie B.," said Mother.

And so then I got very happy inside. Because maybe I didn't have to eat my stewie pewie tomatoes.

And also sometimes a surprise means a present! And presents are my very favorite things in the whole world!

I bounced up and down on my chair.

"What is it? Is it all wrapped up? I don't see it," I said very excited.

Then I looked under the table. Because maybe the surprise was hiding down there with a red ribbon on top of it.

Mother and Daddy smiled at each other. Then Mother held my hand.

"Junie B., how would you like to have a little baby brother or sister?" she said.

I made my shoulders go up and down.

"I don't know. Maybe," I told her.

Then I looked under my chair.

"Guess what?" I said. "I can't find that silly willy present anywhere."

Mother made me sit up. Then she and my daddy said some more stuff about a baby.

"The baby will be yours, too, Junie B.," Daddy said. "Just think. You'll have your very own little brother or sister to play with. Won't that be fun?"

I did my shoulders up and down again. "I don't know. Maybe," I said.

Then I got down from my chair and ran into the living room.

"BAD NEWS, FELLAS!" I hollered very loud. "THE PRESENT ISN'T IN THIS

DUMB BUNNY ROOM, EITHER!"

Mother and Daddy came into the living room. They didn't look that smiley anymore.

Daddy took a big breath. "There is no *present*, Junie B.," he said. "We never said we had a present. We said we had a *surprise*. Remember?"

Then Mother sat down next to me. "The surprise is that I'm going to have a *baby*, Junie B. In a few months you're going to have a little baby brother or sister. Do you get what I'm saying yet?"

Just then I folded my arms and made a grumpy face. 'Cause all of a sudden I got it, that's why.

"You didn't get me a darned thing, did you?" I said very growly.

Mother looked angry at me. "I give up!" she said. Then she went back into the kitchen.

Daddy said that I owed her a 'pology.

A 'pology is when I have to say the words *I'm sorry.*

"Yes, but she owes me a 'pology, too," I said. "Because a baby isn't a very good surprise."

I made a wrinkly nose. "Babies smell like P.U.," I explained. "I smelled one at my friend Grace's house. It had some spit-up on its front. And so I held my nose and hollered, 'P.U.! WHAT A STINK BOMB!' And then that Grace made me go home."

After I finished my story, Daddy went into the kitchen to talk to Mother.

Then Mother called me in there. And she said if the baby smells like a stink bomb, she will buy me my very own air freshener. And I can spray the can all by myself.

Babies smell like P.U.

Except not on the P.U. baby.

"I would like the one that smells as fresh as a Carolina pine forest," I said.

Then me and Mother hugged. And I sat back down at the table. And I finished eating my dinner.

Except not my stewie pewie tomatoes.

And so guess what?

No dessert, that's what.

2 / The Dumb Baby's Room

Mother and Daddy fixed up a room for the new baby. It's called a nursery. Except I don't know why. Because a baby isn't a nurse, of course.

The baby's room used to be the guest room. That's where all our guests used to sleep. Only we never had much guests.

And so now if we get some, they'll have to sleep on a table or something.

The baby's room has new stuff in it. That's because Mother and Daddy went shopping at the new baby stuff store.

They bought a new baby dresser with green and yellow knobs on it. And a new baby lamp with a giraffe on the lamp shade. And also, a new rocking chair for when the baby cries and you can't shut it up.

And there's a new baby crib, too.

A crib is a bed with bars on the side of it. It's kind of like a cage at the zoo. Except with a crib, you can put your hand through the bars. And the baby won't pull you in and kill you.

And guess what else is in the nursery? Wallpaper, that's what! The jungle kind. With pictures of elephants, and lions, and a big fat hippo-pot-of-something.

And there's monkeys, too! Which are my most favorite jungle guys in the whole world!

Mother and Daddy pasted on the wallpaper together.

Me and my dog Tickle were watching them.

"This wallpaper looks very cute in here," I told them. "I would like some of it in my room, too, I think. Okay?" I said. "Can I? Can I?"

"We'll see," said Daddy.

We'll see is another word for no.

"Yeah, only that's not fair," I said. " 'Cause the baby gets all new junk and I have all old junk."

"Poor Junie B.," said Mother very teasing.

Then she bended down and tried to hug me. Only she couldn't do it very good. Because of her big fat stomach—which is where the stupid baby is.

"I don't think I'm going to like this dumb baby," I said.

Mother stopped hugging me.

"Don't say that, Junie B. Of course you will," she said.

"Of course I won't," I talked back. "Because it won't even let me hug you very good. And anyway, I don't even know its stupid dumb name."

Then Mother sat down in the new rocking chair. And she tried to put me on her lap. Only I wouldn't fit. So she just holded my hand.

"That's because Daddy and I haven't picked a name for the baby yet," she explained. "We want a name that's a little bit different. You know, something cute like Junie B. Jones. A name that people will remember."

And so I thought and thought very hard.

And then I clapped my hands together real loud.

"Hey! I know one!" I said very excited. "It's the cafeteria lady at my school. And her name is Mrs. Gutzman!"

Mother frowned a little bit. And so maybe she didn't hear me, I think.

"MRS. GUTZMAN!" I hollered. "That's a cute name, don't you think? And I remembered it, too! Even after I only heard it one time, Mrs. Gutzman sticked right in my head!"

Mother took a big breath. "Yes, honey. But I'm not sure that Mrs. Gutzman is a good name for a tiny baby."

And so then I scrunched my face up. And I thought and thought all over again.

"How 'bout Teeny?" I said. "Teeny would be good."

Mother smiled. "Well, Teeny might be cute while the baby was little. But what would we call him when he grows up?"

"Big Teeny!" I called out very happy.

Then Mother said, "We'll see."

Which means no Big Teeny.

After that, I didn't feel so happy anymore.

"When's this dumb bunny baby getting here anyway?" I said.

Mother frowned again. "The baby is not a dumb bunny, Junie B.," she said. "And it will be here very soon. So I think you'd better start getting used to the idea."

Then her and Daddy began pasting wallpaper again.

And so I opened the new baby dresser with the green and yellow knobs. And I looked at the new baby clothes.

The baby pajamas were very weensy. And the baby socks wouldn't even fit on my big piggie toe.

"I'm going to be the boss of this baby," I said to Tickle. " 'Cause I'm the biggest, that's why."

Daddy snapped his fingers at me. "That's enough of that kind of talk, missy," he said.

Missy's my name when I'm in trouble.

After that, him and Mother went to the kitchen to get some more paste.

And so I looked down the hall to make sure he was gone.

"Yeah, only I'm still gonna be the boss of it," I whispered.

Ha ha. So there.

3 / A Very Wonderful Thing!

Yesterday a very wonderful thing happened!

And it's called—I had pie for dinner!

Just pie and that's all!

That's because my mother went to the hospital to have the baby. And Daddy and Grandma Miller went with her.

And so me and my grampa got to stay at his house. All by ourselves. And no one even babysitted us!

And guess what? Grampa smoked a real live cigar right inside the house! And Grandma didn't yell, "Go outside with that thing, Frank!"

After that, my grampa gave me a piggy-back ride.

And he let me put on Grandma Miller's new hat—with the long brown feather.

And also, I got to walk in her red high heels.

Only then I fell down in the kitchen. And so I quick took them off.

"Hey! I could crack my head open in these dumb things," I said very loud.

After that, I opened up the 'frigerator. 'Cause I was hungry from playing, that's why.

"HEY! GUESS WHAT? THERE'S A BIG FAT LEMON PIE IN HERE, FRANK!" I hollered.

And so then Grampa Miller got down two plates. And then me and him ate the big fat lemon pie for our dinner!!

Just pie and that's all!!

And we're not even going to get in trouble! 'Cause we're going to tell Grandma that her cat ate it!

And here's another very fun thing. I got to sleep in Grampa Miller's guest room!

Lemon pie! Yum! Delicious!

First I put on my p.j.'s with the feet in them. And then my grampa watched me brush my new front tooth. And he tucked me into the big guest bed.

"Sweet dreams, Junie B.," he said.

Except for then I got a little bit of scared in me.

"Yeah. Only guess what, Grampa," I said. "It's very dark in this big room. And so there might be hidey things in here."

Grampa looked all around the room. And also in the closet.

"Nope. No hidey things in here," he said.

After that he left on the hall light for me. So my 'magination wouldn't run wild.

Except I still didn't sleep that good. 'Cause there was a drooly guy with claws under my bed, I think.

And so this morning, my eyes felt very sagging.

Only then I sniffed something that woke them right up.

And its name was delicious waffles!

Grampa Miller cooked them for me! And he let me pour on my own syrup. And he didn't yell whoa! whoa! whoa!

After that, me and him played until it was time for kindergarten.

Except before I left, the funnest thing of all happened! My grandma Miller came home!

And she said that Mother had a baby!

And it was the boy kind!

Then me and her and my grampa all did a big giant hug!

And Grandma Miller picked me up. And she swinged me in the air.

"You're just going to love him, Junie B.!" she said. "Your new brother is the cutest little monkey I've ever seen!"

Then my eyes got very wide. "He is? Really?" I said.

Grandma Miller put me down. Then she started talking to my grampa.

"Wait till you see him, Frank," she said. "He's got the longest little fingers and toes!"

I tugged on her dress. "How long, Grandma?" I said. "Longer than mine?"

But Grandma just kept on talking.

"And his hair, Frank! My word! He's got oodles and oodles of thick black hair!"

I pulled on Grandma's arm. "How come, Grandma? How come he's got hair?" I asked. "I thought little babies were supposed to be baldies."

But still, my grandma didn't answer me.

"And he's big, too, Frank. He's much bigger than any of the other babies in the hospital. And you should feel how tightly he grabs on to your finger when you—"

Just then I stamped my foot very hard.

"HEY! I WANT SOME ANSWERS DOWN HERE, HELEN! HE'S MY BABY TOO, YOU KNOW!"

Grandma Miller frowned at me. 'Cause I'm not supposed to call her Helen, I think.

"Sorry," I said kind of quiet.

Then Grandma Miller bended down next to me. And so I didn't have to yell anymore.

"Are you telling me the truth, Grandma?" I said. "Is my brother *really* the cutest little monkey you ever saw? For really and honest and truly?"

Then my grandma Miller hugged me very tight.

"Yes, little girl," she whispered in my ear. "For really and honest and truly."

After that, she picked me up again. And me and her twirled all around the kitchen.

4 / Hoppy and Russell

My room at kindergarten is named Room Nine.

I have two bestest friends in that place. One of them has the name of Lucille.

Lucille sits right exactly next to me.

She has a red chair. And also little red fingernails which are very glossy.

My other bestest friend is named Grace.

Me and that`Grace sit together on the school bus. Except for not today we didn't. Because today Grampa Miller drove me.

Then he walked to Room Nine with me.

24

And he waved at my teacher.

Her name is Mrs.

She has another name, too. But I just like Mrs. and that's all.

When I first walked into my room, Lucille was looking at that Grace's brand new shoes. And their name was pink high tops.

"Hey, Grace! Those new shoes look very beautiful on you!" I said.

But that dumb Grace didn't even say *thank you* to me.

"Grace is angry at you," said Lucille. "She said that she rode the bus today. And you weren't even there to save her a seat. And she had to sit next to an icky kid. Right, Grace?"

Grace bobbed her head up and down.

"Yes, only I couldn't help it, Grace," I said. "That's because I stayed at my grampa Miller's all night. And there's no bus at that place. And so he had to drive me here today."

Then I tried to hold that Grace's hand. Only she quick pulled it away.

"That's not very nice of you, Grace," I said. "And so guess what? Now I'm not going to tell you my special secret."

That's when that Grace called me a poopy head.

Lucille held my hand. "*I* don't think you're a poopy head, Junie B.," she said. "And so you can tell me your special secret. And I won't tell anybody. Not even Grace."

That's when that Grace kicked Lucille in the leg.

And so Lucille pushed her down.

And Mrs. had to come pull them off each other.

I raised my hand very polite. "I wasn't involved," I said to Mrs.

After that, we had to sit down and do some work. It was called printing our numbers. Only I couldn't do mine that good. Because Lucille kept on talking to me, that's why.

"Come on, Junie B.," she said in her whispering voice. "Tell me your special secret. I won't tell. I promise."

"Yes, only I *can't,* Lucille," I said. " 'Cause no talking to your neighbor, remember?"

Then Mrs. snapped her fingers at me.

"SEE, LUCILLE? I TOLD YOU NO TALKING TO YOUR NEIGHBOR!" I hollered. "NOW I GOT SNAPPED AT!"

Just then a boy named Jim said, "Shush," to me.

"Shush yourself, you big fat Jim," I said back.

After that, Mrs. stood next to me till I

finished my work. Then I got all done and she collected it.

That made me happy inside. Because guess what comes after work? Something very fun, that's what!

And its name is Show and Tell.

Mrs. stood next to her desk. "Who has something interesting to share with the class today?" she said.

Then my heart got very pumpy. Because I had the most special secret in the whole wide world!

I raised my hand way high in the air.

"OOOOOH! OOOOOH!" I hollered real loud. "ME! ME! ME!"

Mrs. shook her head at me. Because I'm not supposed to go oooooh, oooooh, me, me, me.

She called on William. He is a cry-baby

boy in my class. I can beat him up, I think.

"William?" said Mrs. "Since you raised your hand so politely, you may go first."

And so then William carried a paper bag to the front of the room. And he took out a jar of two dead crickets.

Except for William didn't know they were dead. He just thought they were sleeping.

"Jump, Hoppy! Jump, Russell!" said William.

Then he tapped on the glass.

"Hey! Wake up in there!" he said.

After that, William started shaking the jar all over the place. And he wouldn't stop.

"WAKE UP, I SAID!" he shouted.

Then Hoppy and Russell started falling all apart. And Mrs. had to take the jar away.

That's when William started to cry. And he had to go to the nurse's office to lie down.

And so then I raised my hand way high in the air again.

Because guess what? My Show and Tell was *way* better than two dead crickets!

5 / Monkey Business

Mrs. called my name.

"Junie B.? Would you like to go next?" she asked.

Then I jumped right up. And I ran speedy fast to the front of the room.

"Guess what?" I said very excited. "Last night my mother had a baby! And it's the boy kind!"

Mrs. clapped her hands.

"Junie B. Jones has a new little brother, everyone!" she said. "Isn't that wonderful?"

Then all of Room Nine clapped, too.

"Yes, only you haven't even heard the bestest part yet!" I said very loud. "Because guess what else? He's a MONKEY! That's what else! My new brother is a real, alive, baby MONKEY!!!"

Mrs. got a funny look on her face. And she squinted her eyes very tiny. And so maybe she didn't hear me or something, I think.

"I SAID I'VE GOT A MONKEY BROTHER!" I shouted real louder.

Then that mean Jim jumped right up from his desk. And he hollered, "Liar, liar, pants on fire!"

"No they are not on fire, you big fat Jim!" I said back. "I do too have a monkey brother! You can ask my grandma Miller if you don't believe me!"

Mrs. raised her eyebrows way high on her head.

"Your grandmother told you that your brother is a monkey?" she asked me.

"Yes!" I said. "She told me he has long

fingers and long toes. And lots of black fur
all over himself!"

After that, Mrs. kept on looking and
looking at me. Then she said it was time for
me to sit down.

"Yeah, only I'm not done telling the children about my monkey brother yet," I explained.

" 'Cause guess what else? His wallpaper has pictures of his jungle friends on it. And his bed has bars on the sides. But I'm going to teach him not to bite or kill people."

Then this boy named Ricardo—who has cute freckles on his face—said, "Monkeys are cool," to me.

"I know they are cool, Ricardo," I said. "And guess what else? Maybe I can bring him to school on Pet Day."

Then Ricardo smiled at me. And so he might be my boyfriend, I think. Except for there's a boy in Room Eight who already loves me.

Just then, Mrs. stood up and pointed at me.

"That's *enough*, Junie B.," she said. "I want you to sit down now. You and I will talk about this monkey business later."

And so that made me giggle. Because monkey business is a funny word, I think.

Then I waved good-bye to my new boy-friend, Ricardo.

And I skipped back to my seat.

6 / Bestest Friends

Recess is my best subject. I learned it my first week at school.

Recess is when you go outside. And you run off your steam.

Then when you come in, you can sit still better. And you don't have ants in your pants.

At recess, me and Lucille and that Grace play horses together.

I'm Brownie. Lucille is Blackie. And that Grace is Yellowie.

"I'M BROWNIE!" I hollered as soon as I got outside.

"I don't want to play horses today," said Lucille. "I want to know some more about your monkey brother."

"Me, too," said that Grace.

Then Lucille pushed that Grace out of the way. And she whispered a secret in my ear.

"If you let me be the first one to see him, I'll let you wear my new locket," she said.

"Yeah. Only guess what, Lucille?" I said. "I don't even know what a dumb locket is."

And so then Lucille showed me her locket. It was a little gold heart on a chain.

"Isn't it beauteous?" she said. "My nanna gave it to me for my birthday."

Then she opened up the little heart. And there was a little bitty picture inside of that thing!

"Hey! There's a teeny head in there!" I said very excited.

"I know," said Lucille. "That's my nanna. See her?"

I squinted very hard at the little picture.

"Your nanna is a shrimpie, Lucille," I said.

After that, Lucille closed the locket. And she gave it to me.

"Now I'm your best friend, right, Junie B.?" she said. "And so I can be the first one to see your monkey brother!"

Just then, that Grace stomped her foot very hard.

"No you cannot, Lucille!" she hollered. *"I'm* her best friend! 'Cause me and her ride the bus together. And so I get to see her monkey brother first. Right, Junie B.? Right? Right?"

I made my shoulders go up and down.

"I don't know, Grace," I said. " 'Cause Lucille just gave me this locket with the teeny nanna. And so that means she gets to go first, I think."

That Grace stomped her foot again. She made a mad face at me.

"Pooey!" she said.

Except for just then I got a great idea!

"Hey! Guess what, Grace?" I said very excited. "Since Lucille gave me something beautiful, now you can give me something beautiful, too! And so that would be very fair of me, I think!"

Then that Grace started smiling. And she took off her sparkly new ring.

"Here!" she said. "I got it out of cereal this morning! See how shiny the stone is? That's because it's a real genuine fake plastic diamond."

Then she put some breath on it. And she shined it on her sleeve for me.

"Oooooh," I said. "I love this thing, Grace."

"I know," she said. "And so now I get to see your monkey brother first. Right, Junie B.? Right?"

After that I had to think a little bit.

"Yeah, only here's the trouble, Grace," I said. "Now I have one thing from you and one thing from Lucille. And so it's a tie."

Then Lucille quick took off her red sweater with the Scottie dog on it. And she tied it around my waist.

"Here!" she said. "Now I've given you two things! And so I'm still the winner."

"Oh no you're not!" hollered that Grace. "Because I'm gonna give Junie B. my snack ticket for today. And so she can have my cookie and milk!"

"Excellent idea, Grace!" I said.
Then me and her did a high five.

"Oh yeah?" said Lucille. "Well, then I'm going to give her *my* snack ticket, too! And so I'm still the winner!"

After that Grace looked all over herself.

"But that's not fair," she said. "Because I don't have anything else to give her."

And so I looked all over her, too. And then I jumped up and down again.

"Yes you do, Grace!" I said. "You do too have something else to give me! And their name is your new pink high tops!"

That Grace stared at her feet. She looked very sad.

"Yeah, only this is the first time I ever wore these," she said real quiet.

And so I patted her so she would feel better.

"I know, Grace," I explained nicely. "But if you don't give them to me, then you won't be able to see my monkey brother."

And so then me and that Grace sat down on the grass. And she took off her new pink shoes. And she gave them to me.

"Thank you, Grace," I said politely.

Then I stood up.

"Okay. Your turn," I said to Lucille.

Only too bad for me. 'Cause just then the stupid bell rang.

7 / Some School Words

I wore my brand-new things back to Room Nine.

They looked very beautiful on me. Except my new pink high tops were too big. And my feet were very sliding around in there.

Before I sat down I looked at Lucille's red chair. Then I tapped on her.

"I'm sorry, Lucille," I said. "But red is my favorite color. And so I would like that chair of yours, I think."

Lucille looked very upset at me. "But red is my favorite color, too, Junie B."

I patted her. "I know, Lucille," I said nicely. "But you still must give it to me. It's the rules."

And so she did.

"Now I'm the winner for sure, aren't I?" she asked.

I made my shoulders go up and down. "I don't know, Lucille," I said. "That Grace said she might have some cash in her purse."

After that, Mrs. passed out construction paper. And we cut out autumn leaves for our bulletin board.

Autumn is the school word for fall.

We sprinkled our leaves with shiny glitter.

Also, I sprinkled glitter in my hair. And I pasted some to my eyebrows.

Then Mrs. confiscated my shiny glitter jar.

Confiscate is the school word for yanked

47

Autumn is the school word for fall.

it right out of my hand.

Just then, Mrs. Gutzman knocked on our door. And she came into the room with our milk and cookies.

"HURRAY! HURRAY FOR MRS. GUTZMAN!" I shouted at her. "GUESS WHAT, MRS. GUTZMAN? I GET THREE SNACKS TODAY! SEE? I HAVE THREE SNACK TICKETS!"

Mrs. walked over to my chair. She stared down at me.

"How did you get two extra tickets, Junie B.?" she asked. "Did you find them on the playground?"

Then she took my two extra tickets away. And she held them way high in the air.

"Did anyone lose their snack tickets today?" she said to the class.

"NO!" I hollered. "Those are my tickets!

Lucille and Grace gave them to me!"

Mrs. raised her eyebrows. "Lucille? Did you give Junie B. your snack ticket today?" she asked.

"Yes," said Lucille. "That's because she made me."

"No, I did not, you dumb Lucille!" I said. "I did not make you!"

Mrs. said, "Be quiet," to me.

She folded her arms. "Grace? Did you give your snack ticket to Junie B., too?"

Then that Grace started to cry. Because she thought she was in trouble.

Mrs. tapped her foot. "Please come get your snack ticket, Grace," she said.

And so then that Grace walked to my table in just her socks.

And Mrs. made squinty eyes at her feet.

"Where are your shoes, Grace?" she asked.

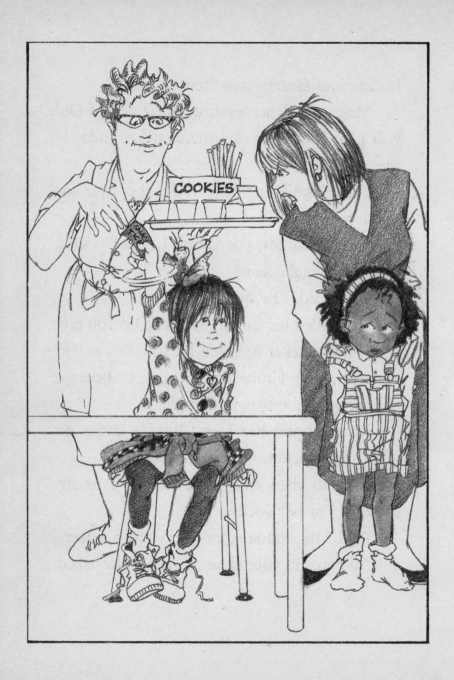

That's when big fat baby Grace started crying very harder. And she pointed at her shoes.

Mrs. peeped under my table.

"Junie B. Jones!" she hollered. "Why are you wearing Grace's shoes?"

Mrs. sounded dangerous.

"Because," I said kind of scared.

"Because why?" said Mrs.

"Because it's the rules," I explained.

Then Mrs. bended down very close to my ear. "What rules?"

"The rules for who gets to be the first one to see my monkey brother," I said.

Mrs. rolled her eyes way back in her head.

"Put your own shoes back on. And come with me, young lady," she said.

Then me and her walked into the hall together. And she made me tell her what happened on the playground.

After that, I had to give Lucille back the locket and the sweater with the Scottie dog on it. And I had to give Grace back the real genuine fake ring from cereal.

Then Mrs. wrote a note. And she said for me to take it to the office.

The office is where the boss of the school lives. His name is Principal.

"Yes, but I don't think I would like to go down there today," I said. "Or else my mother might get mad at me."

Mrs. tapped her foot. Then she took hold of my hand.

"Let's go, young lady. March," she said.

And so then me and her marched to the office.

March is the school word for pulled me way too fast.

8 / Me and Principal

The school office is a scary place.

It has loud ringing phones. And a typing lady who is a stranger. And a row of chairs where bad kids sit.

Mrs. plopped me in a blue one.

"Wait here," she said.

"Yeah, only I'm not bad," I whispered to just myself.

Then I put my sweater on my head. So nobody would see me in the bad kid's chair.

After that, I peeked down my long sweater sleeve. And I saw Mrs. out of my hand hole.

She was knocking on Principal's door.

Then she went in there. And my heart felt very pumpy. Because she was tattle-taling on me, I think.

After a while, she came out again.

Principal came with her.

Principal has a baldy head which looks like rubber.

Also, he has big hands. And heavy shoes. And a suit made out of black.

"Could I see you in my office for a minute, Junie B.?" he said.

And so then I had to go in there all by myself. And I sat in a big wood chair. And Principal made me take the sweater off my head.

"So what's this all about?" he said. "Why do you think your teacher brought you down here today?"

"Because," I said very quiet.

"Because why?" said Principal.

"Because that Grace shot off her big fat mouth," I explained.

Then Principal folded his arms. And he said for me to start at the beginning.

And so I did. . . .

First, I told him about how I spent the night at my grampa's house.

"We had delicious waffles for breakfast," I said. "And I had five of them. Only my grampa didn't know where I put them all. Except I put them way in here."

Then I opened my mouth and showed Principal where my waffles went.

After that, I told him how my grandma Miller came home from the hospital. And she told me I had a monkey brother. For really and honest and truly.

"And so then I told the children at Show

and Tell," I said. "And at recess Lucille and that Grace started giving me lots of pretty stuff. Because they wanted to be first to see him.

"Except too bad for me," I said. "Because when we came inside, Mrs. found out about the snack tickets. And then that dumb Grace shot off her big fat mouth about her shoes. And so I got marched down here. And I had to sit in the bad kid's chair."

Then I smoothed my skirt. "The end," I said nicely.

Principal rubbed his head that looks like rubber.

"Junie B., maybe we should go back to when your grandmother came home from the hospital," he said. "Can you remember *exactly* what she said about your brother being a monkey?"

I scrunched my eyes real tight to remember.

"Yes," I said. "Grandma Miller said he was the cutest little monkey she ever saw."

Then Principal closed his eyes. "Aaah," he said kind of quiet. "Now I get it."

After that, he smiled a little bit. "You see, Junie B., when your grandmother called your brother a little monkey, she didn't mean he was a *real* little monkey. She just meant he was, well . . . cute."

"I know he's cute," I said. "That's because all monkeys are cute. Except for I don't like the big kind that can kill you."

Principal shook his head. "No, Junie B., that's not what I mean. I mean your brother isn't really a monkey at all. He's just a little baby boy."

I made a frowny face. "No, he is *not* a

little baby boy," I told him. "He's a real, alive, baby monkey with black hairy fur and long fingers and toes. You can ask my grandma Miller if you don't believe me."

And so guess what Principal did then? He called her, that's what! He called Grandma Miller right up on the phone!

And then he talked to her. And then I talked to her too!

"Hey, Grandma!" I said very shouty. "Guess what just happened down here? Principal said that my baby brother isn't a real, alive monkey. Only he is. 'Cause you told me that. Remember? You said he was a monkey. For really and honest and truly."

Then Grandma Miller said she was very sorry. But she didn't mean he was a *real* monkey. She just meant he was *cute*.

Just like Principal explained to me.

And so then I felt very droopy inside.

"Yeah, only what about all of his black hair? And his long fingers and toes?" I said. "And what about his bed that looks like a cage? And the wallpaper with his jungle friends on it?"

But Grandma Miller kept on saying that my new brother was just a regular cute baby. And so finally I didn't want to talk to her anymore. And I hanged up the phone.

Then I bended my head way down. And my eyes got a little bit of wet in them.

"Darn it," I said very quiet.

After that, Principal gave me a tissue. And he said, "I'm sorry," to me.

Then he held my hand.

And me and him walked back to Room Nine.

9 / Pigs and Ducks and Stuff

Principal went into Room Nine with me.

Then he clapped his giant hands together.

"Boys and girls? May I please have your attention?" he said. "I would like to explain what happened during Show and Tell today. It's about Junie B. Jones and her new baby brother."

Just then that Jim I hate jumped right up out of his chair.

"He's not a monkey, is he?" he shouted very loud. "I knew it! I knew he wasn't a monkey!"

I made a big fist at him. "HOW WOULD YOU LIKE THIS UP YOUR NOSE, YOU BIG DUMB JIM?" I hollered.

Then Principal frowned at me. And so I smiled.

"I hate that guy," I said nicely.

After that, Principal took a big breath.

"Boys and girls, there's a good reason why Junie B. told you that her baby brother was a monkey," he said.

"Yeah! It was all my grandma Miller's fault!" I interrupted. "Because she told me that my brother was a *little monkey*. Only she didn't mean he was a *real* little monkey. She just meant he was cute. Only who the heck knew that dumb thing?"

Principal made another frown at me. Then he talked some more.

"You see, boys and girls," he said. "Sometimes adults say things that can be very confusing to children. Like what if you heard me talking about a *lucky duck?* You might think I was talking about a real live duck. But *lucky duck* just means a lucky person."

"Right," said Mrs. "And when we call someone a *busy bee,* we don't mean he's a real bee. We just mean he's a hard worker."

"Hey! I just thought of another one!" I said very excited. "A dumb bunny isn't a real alive bunny, either! It's just a plain old dumb guy!"

Then my friend Lucille raised her hand.

"I've got one, too," she said. "Sometimes my nanna calls my daddy a couch potato. Only he's not a real potato. He's just a lazy bum."

"Yeah, and I'm not a big pig," said my new boyfriend Ricardo. "But my mom says I eat like one."

After that, a whole bunch of other kids said they eat like big pigs, too.

Only a boy named Donald said he eats like a horse.

And crybaby William eats like a bird.

Just then it was time for the bell to ring. And so me and Principal said bye-bye to each other. And I went to my seat.

Then I gave Lucille back her red chair. She was very nice to me.

"I'm sorry that your brother isn't a real monkey, Junie B.," she said.

"Thank you, Lucille," I said. "I'm sorry that your daddy isn't a real potato, too."

After that, the bell rang for us to go home.

And so me and Lucille and that Grace held hands. And we walked outside together.

Only then a very wonderful thing happened!

And it's called—I heard my mother's voice!

"JUNIE B.! JUNIE B.! OVER HERE, HONEY. DADDY AND I ARE OVER HERE!"

Then I looked in the parking lot. And I saw her! And so I runned to her speedy quick. And then me and Mother hugged and hugged. Because I hadn't seen her for a very whole day!

Then my daddy got out of the car. And he had a little yellow blanket in his arms. And guess what was in that thing?

My new baby brother, that's what!

He was very teeny. And pinkish. Except his head had a lot of black hair on it.

I touched it. It felt like fuzzy.

Just then Ricardo walked by. And he saw my teeny brother.

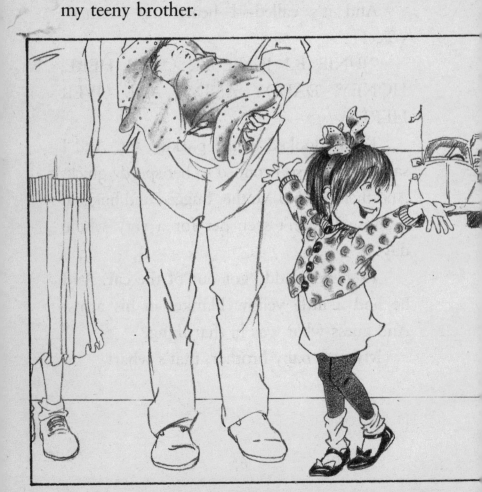

"Cool hair," he said.

I smiled very big. "I know it, Ricardo," I said. "And guess what else? He doesn't even smell like P.U."

After that I got in the car. And I told

Mother about Lucille's locket. And she said maybe I could get a locket, too. And I could put my brother's teeny head in there.

"Yes. And I would also like some pink high tops, please," I said very polite.

"Maybe," said Mother.

"Oh boy!" I said.

'Cause *maybe* doesn't mean no! That's why!

And so then I lifted up the blanket. And I peeped at my baby brother one more time.

"So what do you think of him, Junie B.?" said Mother.

I smiled very big. "I think he's the cutest little monkey I ever saw," I said.

Then Mother laughed.

And I laughed, too.

Junie B. Jones

Junie B.'s Sticker Scrapbook Sensation to Spark Your 'Magination!
(Psst! And It's FREE!)

Do You Want . . .

- a special book to save your favorite Junie B. stickers from the new foil-covered paperbacks?
- a perfect place to paste and draw your memories from this year?
- lots of happy, creative scrapbook tips from Junie B.?

YES! YES! YES!

(You can get it FREE at participating retailers and online at www.randomhouse.com/junieb)

Here are some of Junie B.'s favorite photos from her *own* sticker scrapbook!

Bestest Good Friends!

Uh-oh! I'm in Trouble!

Wowie wow wow!
I'm so glad you're my pal!
Let's play at my Web site.
I'll meet you there now!

www.randomhouse.com/kids/junieb

Don't miss these other great books
by Barbara Park!

Rah! Rah! Rah!
Join the crowd.
Read these books
And laugh out loud!

Junie B. has a lot to say
about everything and everybody . . .

the baby's room
Mother and Daddy fixed up a room for the new baby. It's called a nursery. Except I don't know why. Because a baby isn't a nurse, of course.
- from *Junie B. Jones and a Little Monkey Business*

school words
After that, the mop got removed from us. *Removed* is the school word for snatched right out of our hands.
- from *Junie B. Jones and Her Big Fat Mouth*

rules
Me and Mother had a little talk. It was called—*no screaming back off, clown.* Only I never even heard of that rule before.
- from *Junie B. Jones and the Yucky Blucky Fruitcake*

her baby brother
His name is Ollie. I love him a real lot. Except I wish he didn't live at my actual house.
- from *Junie B. Jones and That Meanie Jim's Birthday*

... in Barbara Park's
Junie B. Jones books!

saving a seat
Saving a seat is when you zoom on the bus. And you hurry up and sit down. And then you quick put your feet on the seat next to you. After that, you keep on screaming the word "SAVED! SAVED! SAVED!" And no one even sits next to you. 'Cause who wants to sit next to a screamer? That's what I would like to know.
• from *Junie B. Jones Loves Handsome Warren*

twirling
I twirled and twirled all over the kitchen. Only too bad for me. 'Cause I accidentally twirled into the refrigerator and the stove and the dishwasher.
• from *Junie B. Jones Is a Beauty Shop Guy*

cribs
A crib is a bed with bars on the side of it. It's kind of like a cage at the zoo. Except with a crib, you can put your hand through the bars. And the baby won't pull you in and kill you.
• from *Junie B. Jones and a Little Monkey Business*

Books are my very FAVORITE things in the whole world! I have *lots* of funny stories to share! Laugh out loud with books like these. . . .